Chris RIDDELL

Ottoline
at
Sea

MACMILLAN CHILDREN'S BOOKS

For my nephew, Stephen

Chris Riddell

1. Lives by the seaside in Brighton with his wife and three children.

2. Writes and illustrates books like these by himself, and books like these with Paul Stewart.

The Emperor of Absurdia • Wendel's Workshop • Ottoline and the Yellow Cat • Ottoline goes to School • Ottoline at Sea • The Blobheads • MUDDLE EARTH • THE EDGE CHRONICLES

3. Draws a cartoon every Sunday for the Observer newspaper.

4. Has two of these in a box where he keeps his treasures

and four of these on his son Jack's bookshelf. →

KATE GREENAWAY MEDAL for Pirate Diary • KATE GREENAWAY MEDAL for Gulliver

SMARTIES GOLD AWARD FOR FERGUS CRANE • NESTLÉ SILVER AWARD FOR CORBY FLOOD • NESTLÉ SILVER AWARD FOR HUGO PEPPER • NESTLÉ SILVER AWARD FOR THE EMPEROR OF ABSURDIA

5. His Dad's first car was an Armstrong Siddley (if you'd like to know more, visit www.panmacmillan.com/chrisriddell)

THE Ottoline Books

NESTLÉ CHILDREN'S BOOK PRIZE GOLD MEDAL

WINNER SHEFFIELD CHILDREN'S BOOK AWARD
SHORTER NOVELS CATEGORY

WINNER RED HOUSE CHILDREN'S BOOK AWARD FOR YOUNGER READERS

WINNER LINCOLNSHIRE YOUNG PEOPLE'S BOOK AWARD

WINNER HIGHLAND CHILDREN'S BOOK AWARD

SHORTLISTED FOR THE CILIP KATE GREENAWAY MEDAL

BIG CITY LITERARY GOBLET FOR BOOKS ABOUT HAIRY NORWEG BOG PEOPLE

QUOTES

'Beautifully illustrated'
Guardian

'Each page is designed with retro elegance'
Sunday Times

Look out for more adventures with OTTOLINE

Ottoline and the Yellow Cat

Ottoline goes to School

Chapter One

Ottoline lived on the twenty-fourth floor of the Pepperpot Building. It was on 3rd Street, which had Gruberman's Korean Theatre at one end and Pettigrew Park and Ornamental Gardens at the other. In the middle was the 3rd Street Shoe Store.

THE PEPPERPOT BUILDING

THE POINTY TOWER

OTTOLINE'S APARTMENT

THE SHOEBOX BUILDING

THE ICE-CREAM CONE BUILDING

THE 3rd ST SHOE STORE

THE 3rd ST PENCIL BOUTIQUE

THE 3rd ST ICE-CREAM PARLOUR

3RD STREET

Ottoline lived in Apartment 243 with Mr. Munroe, who was small and hairy and didn't like the rain or having his hair brushed.

Ottoline and Mr. Munroe were good at solving tricky problems and working out clever plans, which they did quite a lot . . .

Like the time they caught the notorious jewel thief the Yellow Cat . . .

YOU CAN READ ABOUT IT IN "OTTOLINE AND THE YELLOW CAT"

YOU CAN READ ABOUT THE GHOST IN "OTTOLINE GOES TO SCHOOL"

. . . and the time they came face to face with the ghost of the Horse of the Hammersteins.

But whatever Ottoline and Mr. Munroe did, they did it together.

The Whistle of the Wild
TALES OF ANIMAL HITCHHIKING
Thør Thørenssen

One morning at the beginning of the school
holidays . . .

That afternoon Ottoline and and Mr. Munroe
were walking down 3rd Street when a
large billboard caught Mr. Munroe's eye.
He stopped and pointed.

"Not now, Mr. Munroe," said Ottoline
absent-mindedly. "When we go on holiday
I'm going to need some shoes . . ."

NORWAY

LAND OF BOGS AND BEAUTY

3RD ST.

"Bonjour, Ottoline!" said Vivienne of the
3rd Street Shoe Store. "I see you've spotted
the Penguin Slippers. I also have your size
in the Eskimo Pumps, the Caribou Platforms
and a pair of quite unusual Moose Boots."

"I'll take them all," said Ottoline. "You
can't have too many shoes on holiday. Could
you tie them in a parcel with lots of string,
please?"

THE POLAR BEAR SHOE Cº

ESKIMO PUMPS

MOOSE BOOTS

CARIBOU PLATFORMS

PENGUIN SLIPPERS

That evening Ottoline and Mr. Munroe sat
down to dinner. Ottoline had macaroni cheese
and lime-juice cordial, freshly delivered to the
table by the Home-Cooked Meal Company.
Mr. Munroe had a bowl of porridge and a mug
of hot chocolate, which is what he always had.

LOTS OF
PEOPLE
LOOK
AFTER
OTTOLINE.
THESE ARE
THEIR
BUSINESS
CARDS

Mr. Munroe was just about to sip his hot chocolate when . . .

. . . he noticed something rather unusual.
He rushed down to Ottoline's end of the table.

"Don't make a mess, Mr. Munroe," said Ottoline distractedly. She was busy rereading her favourite book, *The Whistle of the Wild - Tales of Animal Hitchhiking* by Thør Thørenssen, to get some ideas for where to go on holiday. She had just got to the bit about being polite to llamas.

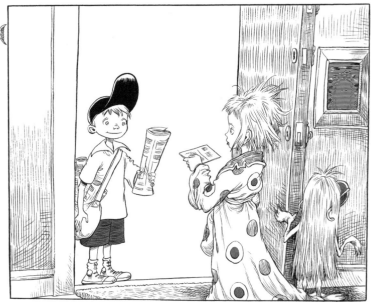

The following morning Max the paper boy
delivered the *Big City Enquirer* to Apartment
243. Ottoline was reading the postcard that
she'd just found on the welcome mat.

"Going somewhere nice for the holidays?"
he asked.

"I haven't decided," said Ottoline. She
began flicking through the newspaper. "Yet."

THIS IS
THE
POSTCARD

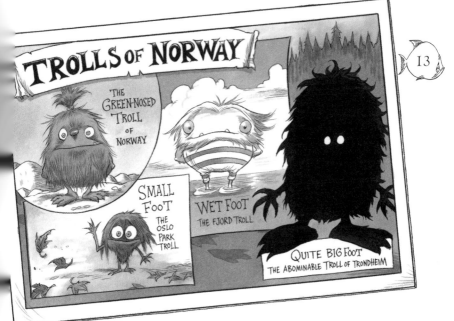

TROLLS OF NORWAY

THE GREEN-NOSED TROLL OF NORWAY

SMALL FOOT
THE OSLO PARK TROLL

WET FOOT
THE FJORD TROLL

QUITE BIG FOOT
THE ABOMINABLE TROLL OF TRONDHEIM

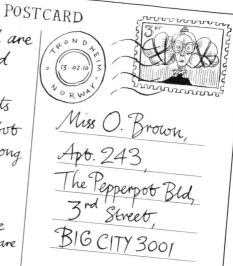

POSTCARD

Dearest O,
Pa and Z are troll spotting and Pa thought he'd found the footprints of "Quite Big Foot" but they turned out to belong to a dancing eek!
lots of love,
Ma.
P.S. You and Mr. Monroe should have a holiday. We are sending a parcel.

TRONDHEIM
13·02·10
NORWAY

3 kr

Miss O. Brown,
Apt. 243,
The Pepperpot Bld,
3rd Street,
BIG CITY 3001

14 For the rest of the day Mr. Munroe kept seeing strange and unusual things.

McBEAN'S CLEANING SERVICE

SMITH & SMITH PILLOW-PLUMPING AND CURTAIN-DRAWING TECHNICIANS

MARION'S BATHROOM SUPPLIES

THE SMILING DRAGON CLOTHES FOLDING Co

Nobody else did. They were all too busy . . .

Mr. Munroe felt sad.

But Ottoline didn't notice.

Chapter Two

"Just going down to do the laundry!"
called Ottoline later that evening.
Mr. Munroe didn't hear her.

In the basement a large bear was sorting through a pile of clothes.

"Hello," Ottoline said. "You are just the bear to talk to. I am thinking of taking Mr. Munroe on holiday. He could do with a change of scene."

"What a good idea," said the bear. "Anywhere nice?"

"Somewhere hot and sunny," said Ottoline. "Mr. Munroe doesn't like getting cold or wet."

She picked up a basket of clean laundry. "Have you seen my stripy socks?"

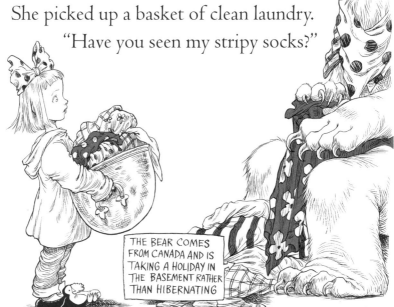

THE BEAR COMES FROM CANADA AND IS TAKING A HOLIDAY IN THE BASEMENT RATHER THAN HIBERNATING

Mr. Munroe climbed to the top of the fire escape and on to the roof of the Pepperpot Building, which is where he always went when he needed to be alone. Except that evening he didn't stop there . . .

Mr. Munroe carried on up the dome of the
pepper pot . . .

. . . right to the very top, higher than he'd ever climbed before.

25

"Pahang is very sunny at this time of year," the bear said, passing Ottoline a floral handkerchief.

OTTOLINE LIKES LISTENING TO THE PIPES IN THE BASEMENT CEILING AND HEARING INTERESTING CONVERSATIONS IN OTHER APARTMENTS IN THE PEPPERPOT BUILDING

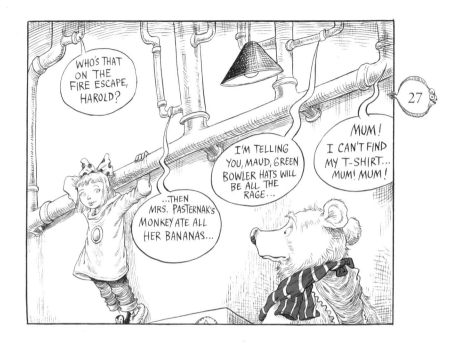

"I could visit my friend the Sultana," said Ottoline. "She has a hairy elephant called Bye-Bye."

"Sounds lovely," said the bear. "I could help you pack." He folded a pair of polka-dot knickerbockers. "Will you be eavesdropping this evening?"

"Only for a little bit," said Ottoline.

Ottoline and the bear went back up to
Apartment 243.

"Mr. Munroe!" called Ottoline excitedly,
knocking on the door to his room. "I know
the perfect place to go on holiday! The
bear has come to help us pack and . . ." She
stopped.

Mr. Munroe's room was empty.

"Where is he?" asked Ottoline with tears in her eyes. "It's not like Mr. Munroe to go anywhere without telling me. And look! He's taken his duffel bag . . ."

She began to cry.

Just then Mrs. Pasternak and her pet monkey, Morris, from Apartment 244 came in. "The front door was open, Ottoline, dear," she said. "Is everything all right?"

"No!" sobbed Ottoline. "Mr. Munroe has disappeared and I don't know where he is."

"I think I do," said Mrs. Pasternak.

Chapter Three

"Mr. Munroe was obviously trying to tell you something, dear," Mrs. Pasternak said as she poured them all another cup of tea from the four-spouted teapot.

"Yes. It must be my fault Mr. Munroe has gone to Norway all by himself," said Ottoline tearfully. The bear offered her a large spotted handkerchief.

"There, there, dear," said Mrs. Pasternak sympathetically. "Worse things happen at sea. What you need is a good night's sleep. I'm sure things will seem better in the morning."

But that night Ottoline couldn't sleep.
She lay wide awake, thinking about
Mr. Munroe . . .

. . . and missing him.

In the morning Ottoline found a postcard and
a brown-paper parcel on the doormat.

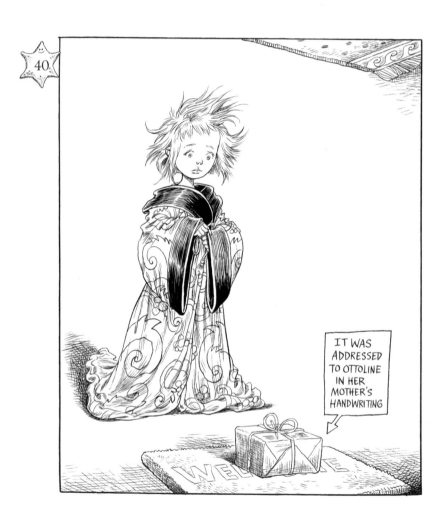

IT WAS
ADDRESSED
TO OTTOLINE
IN HER
MOTHER'S
HANDWRITING

THESE WERE INSIDE

ROVING COLLECTORS'
TRAVEL
PASS

PERMITS *Ottoline Brown*
AND ASSISTANT TO ROVE FOR 17 DAYS
ONLY

LOOK THROUGH HERE

PRESS THIS BUTTON

ROVE O'MATIC

TRAVEL CAMERA

PHOTOGRAPH COMES OUT HERE

Ottoline rushed to the cupboard where the bear liked to sleep.

"Wake up!" she said. "I'm going to Norway to find Mr. Munroe! Will you come as my assistant?"

"I'd be delighted," said the bear.

THE CUPBOARD IS FULL OF ROVING COLLECTORS' CLOTHES

Ottoline knocked on the door of Apartment 244. "Good morning, Mrs. Pasternak!" she said. "You were right, things do seem better. We're going to Norway to find Mr. Munroe! Could you give us a lift to Big City Harbour?"

"Oh, I think I can do better than that," said Mrs. Pasternak mysteriously.

Ten minutes later they were driving down 3rd Street in Mrs. Pasternak's Warren-Harding Continental. The automobile was so big that Mrs. Pasternak couldn't see over the steering wheel and had to look through it instead. Morris the monkey stuck his head out of the window and gave hand signals.

Mrs. Pasternak drove past all the ships that were moored, right the way to the very end of the dock, until Morris waved STOP!

Mrs. Pasternak walked down to the edge of
the dock and peered into Big City Harbour's
murky waters.

"Cooo-eeee! Jules!" she called. "It's Aunt
Judy. I hope this isn't an inconvenient time . . ."

A moment later a tall periscope appeared.

Mrs. Pasternak waved. "Sorry to bother you, dear," she said.

The periscope disappeared back into the water, which began to swirl and bubble . . .

. . . and a small, slightly rusty-looking green submarine rose to the surface. A hatch opened and four heads appeared.

"This is my nephew, Captain Jules Pasternak," said Mrs. Pasternak proudly, "and his crew: Derek, Phoebe and Nugent."

"Hello, Aunt Judy," said Captain Pasternak. "What can I do for you?"

51

"My next-door neighbour, Ottoline Brown, and her assistant want to go to Norway," Mrs. Pasternak explained. "Can you help, Jules, dear?"

"An Amateur Roving Collector, eh?" said Captain Pasternak, looking at Ottoline's travel pass and stroking his beard thoughtfully. "I have a few errands to run and some underwater exploring to do, but I can take you some of the way," he said. "And with your travel pass you should be able to pick up another lift."

"Thank you," said Ottoline, climbing aboard.

THE

THIS IS THE VIEW THROUGH THE PERISCOPE

53

"Take care," called Mrs. Pasternak from the dock, waving an embroidered handkerchief, "and remember to wear a vest!"

"Aye aye!" called Ottoline as the *Iron Leviathan* headed out to sea.

"Batten down the hatches," ordered Captain Pasternak in a cheerful voice, "and prepare to dive!"

55

THE CAPTAIN'S CABIN

THE GALLEY

STORES

THE
IRON LEVIATHAN

Ottoline and the bear got settled into their
hammocks as the *Iron Leviathan* went deeper
and deeper under the sea.

"I miss Mr. Munroe," said Ottoline sadly.

"I know it won't be the same," said the bear,
"but I packed a hairbrush . . ."

"Why Norway of all places?" Ottoline
mumbled to herself as she brushed the
bear's fur. "Mr. Munroe doesn't like the cold
and rain . . ."

"Ah! Unless, of course, he wants to help Ma and Pa look for Quite Big Foot . . ."

"Quite Big Foot the Abominable Troll?!" exclaimed Captain Pasternak. "Terrifying creature, by all accounts. Eight foot tall, and with a temper to match! But very hard to find, a little like mermaids . . ."

"Mermaids?" said Ottoline.

"Yes," said Captain Pasternak. "Would you care to take a look?"

"Yes, please," said Ottoline. She looked through the periscope.

"I can't see any mermaids," said Ottoline.

"Exactly," said Captain Pasternak, taking a deep-sea diving suit off a hook. "Time for a closer inspection."

Chapter Four

61

64

68

On-board the *Iron Leviathan*, Derek, Phoebe and Nugent helped Ottoline into a deep-sea diving suit.

"It really suits you," said the bear.

"Ready to look for mermaids?" said Captain Pasternak in a rather muffled voice.

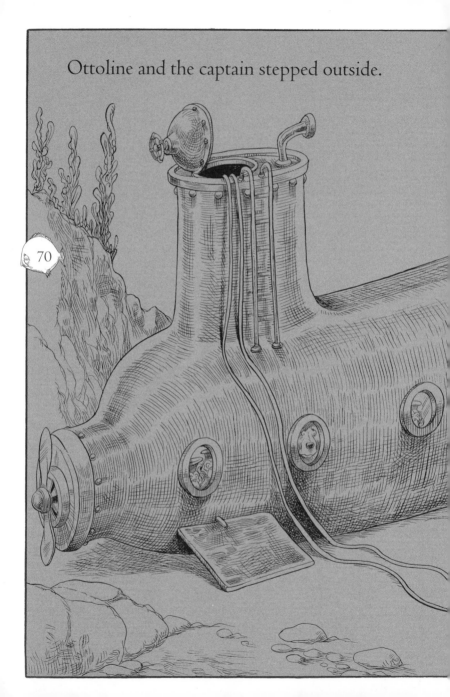

Ottoline and the captain stepped outside.

70

Ottoline thought she'd caught a glimpse of something interesting and wanted to investigate, but they had reached the limit of their oxygen pipes and couldn't go any further. So they turned round and went back to the *Iron Leviathan*.

"No mermaids today," said Captain Pasternak in a gurgling underwater voice. "Underwater exploration is like that — you never know what's around the next corner."

Chapter Five

79

81

83

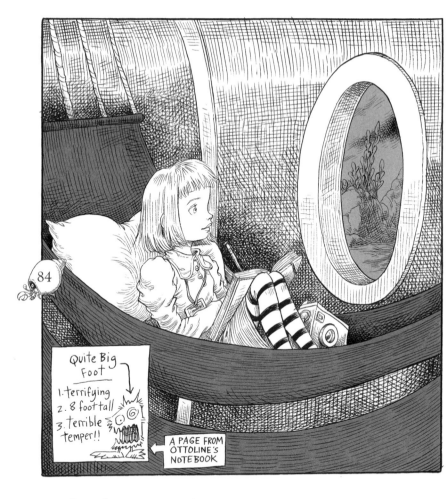

Ottoline was making some Amateur Roving
Collectors' notes in her notebook, when there
was a tap-tap-tapping sound at the porthole.

85

Ottoline looked up. Quickly she grabbed the
Rove O'Matic travel camera and started taking
photographs.

87

THESE ARE
OTTOLINE'S
PHOTOGRAPHS

Ottoline was busy sticking the photographs of the mermaid into her notebook when the bear came out of the captain's cabin.

"The captain's given me his second-best uniform coat," he said proudly. "What do you think?"

Ottoline smiled. "It suits you," she said.

Ottoline took her notebook to Captain
Pasternak to show him her photographs.

Captain Pasternak was sitting at his desk,
drawing pictures of imaginary mermaids.

"What have you got there?" he asked.
Just then an alarm sounded.

"What's that?" said the bear. "Are we there yet?"

"I don't think so . . ." said Ottoline, looking out of a porthole.

"Nothing to worry about," said Captain Pasternak. "That's just the Iceberg Warning Alarm."

"Iceberg Warning Alarm?" said the bear.

"Yes," said Captain Pasternak cheerfully. "It warns you when you're about to hit a massive iceberg."

BEEP! BEEP! BEEP!

"Hold tight!" shouted Captain Pasternak, seizing the submarine's helm. "Crew, prepare to surface!"

Everyone slid to the stern of the submarine, except for Captain Pasternak, who was holding on tightly to the helm, and Nugent, who was swinging from the periscope.

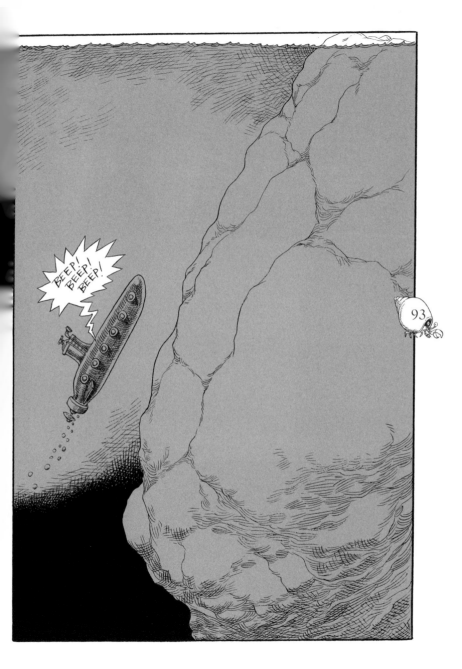

The *Iron Leviathan* surfaced just in time to avoid hitting the massive iceberg.

Captain Pasternak opened the hatch and everyone looked out.

"Hello," said some polar bears. "We were wondering when you'd show up."

Chapter Six

"Come inside," said one of the polar bears. "You're just in time for tea."

"Inside?" said Ottoline.

"Yes," said the polar bear, pointing towards the mouth of an icy cave. "This is just the tip of the iceberg."

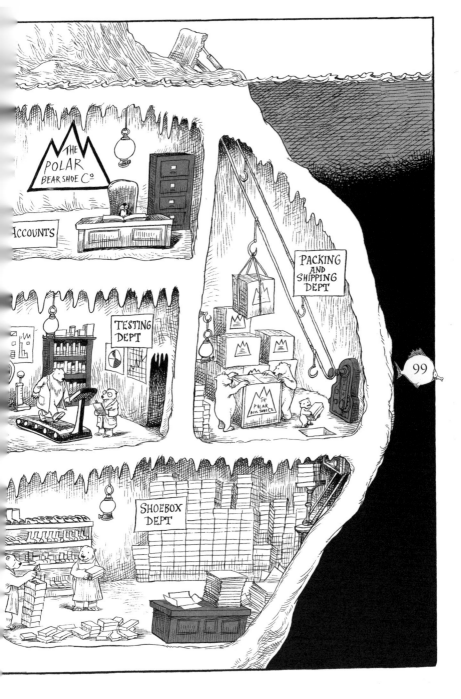

THE POLAR BEAR SHOE Cº

ACCOUNTS

PACKING AND SHIPPING DEPT

TESTING DEPT

SHOEBOX DEPT

99

"Welcome to the Polar Bear Shoe Company," said one of the polar bears. "My name's Libby."

"I have some of your shoes in my Odd Shoe collection!" Ottoline said excitedly. "I love your Penguin Slippers."

While Captain Pasternak and the crew of the *Iron Leviathan* unloaded supplies, Libby gave Ottoline and the bear a tour of the iceberg.

Stephen showed Ottoline a design he was working on. "It's called the Polar Choo-Choo Shoe."

Ottoline was very impressed.

ANNE AND STEPHEN IN DESIGN

Paul and Julie showed them some of their fun fur. "None of it comes from real animals," said Paul.

PAUL AND JULIE
IN FUN FUR

DAVE AND IZZY
IN SEWING AND GLUING

RICHARD AND URSULA
IN SHOE BOXES

Richard and Ursula worked in the Shoebox Department. "I love shoeboxes," said Ottoline. "Shoeboxes are my life," said Richard.

"Jeremy and Alice test all our shoes," said Libby. "For comfort, warmth and personality."

"Personality?" said the bear.

"You wouldn't want a shoe without personality," said Alice, ticking a box on her clipboard.

JEREMY AND ALICE
IN TESTING

CONRAD, SARAH AND
OSCAR IN PACKING AND
SHIPPING

102

McNally worked in Accounts. McNally stared at Ottoline but didn't say anything.

MCNALLY
IN
ACCOUNTS

"Penguins have a natural talent for numbers," said Libby, "but they don't say much."

"Where are you travelling to?" asked
Libby when they had finished the tour. The
Iron Leviathan had been loaded with shoes for
Big City and was ready to leave.

"Norway," said Ottoline.

"Land of Bogs and Beauty," said Libby
thoughtfully. "Well, you'll certainly need a
pair of these," she said, picking up a pair of
enormous wellington boots.

"They're a little big for me," said Ottoline,
"but I'll grow into them. Thank you very much."

Everybody from the Polar Bear Shoe
Company came to the tip of the iceberg and
waved goodbye.

"Thank you for the tea and the tour!"
called Ottoline.

"We've got to get these shoes to Big City," said Captain Pasternak, "but I'm sure my good friend Minty Woodvine of the Arctic Mail will give you a lift."

Ottoline heard a droning sound and, looking up, saw a green seaplane in the sky above. It circled the *Iron Leviathan* three times and then came in to land on the water.

108

Chapter Seven

"Ahoy there!" said the pilot of the seaplane. "Fancy flying into you, Captain Pasternak."

"This is Ottoline Brown and her assistant. They're on their way to Norway," the captain said.

"An Amateur Roving Collector, I see," said Minty Woodvine when Ottoline showed her her travel pass. "Well, this is your lucky day because Norway is on my route. Climb aboard."

"Thank you," said Ottoline, who was very impressed with Minty's long green hair.

"Fasten seat belts and prepare for take-off," said Minty Woodvine as she fired up the seaplane's engines.

"Goodbye, and thank you, Captain Pasternak," Ottoline called as the seaplane took to the skies.

113

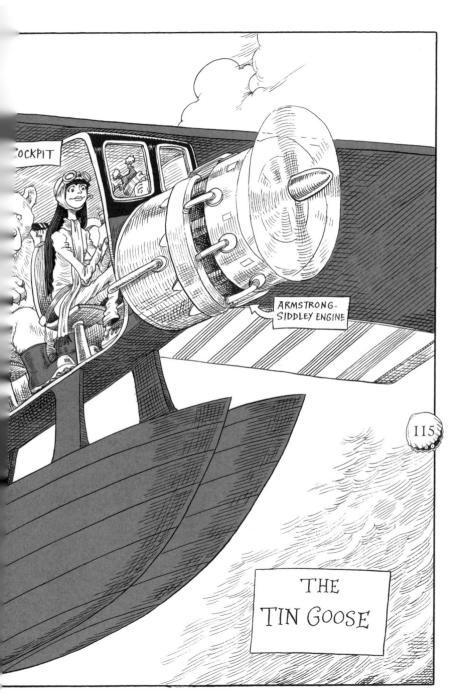

COCKPIT

ARMSTRONG-SIDDLEY ENGINE

115

THE
TIN GOOSE

After a while the blue sky began to turn dark, and ominous-looking clouds began to gather around them . . .

. . . getting bigger and blacker the further they flew.

"It might get a little bumpy," said Minty cheerfully.

First of all it was a little bit bumpy . . .

117

. . . then it got very bumpy.

"So, why Norway, Land of Bogs and Beauty?" said Minty Woodvine brightly.

"I'm trying to find my best friend, Mr. Munroe," said Ottoline, trying not to look out of the window as the seaplane lurched to one side. "I think he's gone to Norway to help my parents look for Quite Big Foot—"

"The Abominable Troll of Trondheim?" said Minty in a shocked voice. "I hear it's eight feet tall, with claws like toasting forks and eyes as bright as headlamps and twice as scary! Why would anyone want to look for it?"

"Ma and Pa are Professional Roving Collectors," said Ottoline. "They're always on the lookout for interesting things."

"Well, I hope for their sakes they don't find it!" said Minty, shaking her head.

Just then there was a loud bang followed by a clunking sound.

"Hold tight!" shouted Minty. "Looks like we're in for a splash landing."

The seaplane swooped down out of the storm clouds towards the sea below.

Ottoline held on to the bear's paw and shut her eyes.

Everything went very, very quiet and then there was a tremendous . . .

121

Chapter Eight

O ttoline opened her eyes and looked out of the cabin window. The seaplane was bobbing about in the water next to a rocky island with a small wood on it.

Two green-nosed trolls came out
from the trees.

"I'm George and this is Ringo," said the first
green-nosed troll.

"I'm Ringo and this is George," said the
second.

"The flange bolt needs reflanging," said
Minty, getting out her toolbox. "And the
spatch lock needs unspatching. This might
take some time . . ."

"Stay as long as you like," said George.

"This is a very small Norwegian wood,
and we don't get many visitors," said Ringo.
"Come inside for breakfast – we're having
pancakes and herring."

THE
NORWEGIAN
WOOD

125

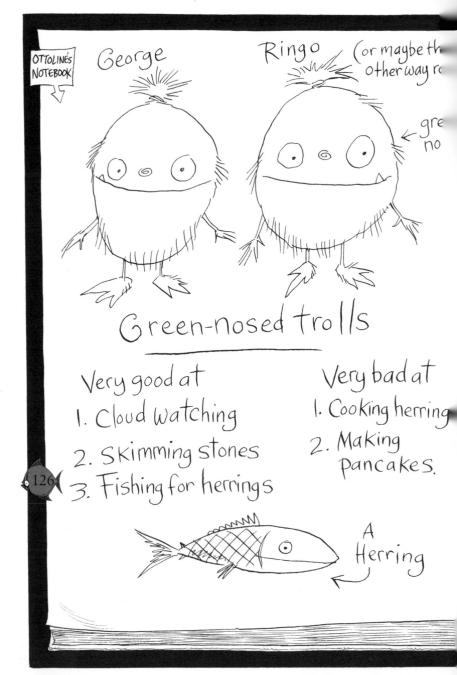

OTTOLINE'S
NOTEBOOK

George

Ringo

(or maybe th...
other way r...

gre...
no...

Green-nosed trolls

Very good at
1. Cloud watching
2. Skimming stones
3. Fishing for herrings

Very bad at
1. Cooking herring...
2. Making
    pancakes.

126

A
Herring

Quite Big Foot

1. 8 foot tall
2. Claws like toasting forks
3. Eyes like head lamps
4. Tangly hair
5. Snaggly teeth
6. TERRIFYING!

127

Later that afternoon, while Minty worked on the seaplane, the bear did some laundry and the green-nosed trolls skimmed stones, Ottoline sat down on a rock by the shore with her notebook.

She'd just finished drawing a sketch of Quite Big Foot when she looked up and saw a raft approaching. It looked very familiar.

128

129

"Thør Thørrensen, the famous explorer!" she exclaimed excitedly. "*The Whistle of the Wild – Tales of Animal Hitchhiking* is my favourite book!"

"Why, thank you," said Thør Thørrensen as he guided his Polynesian raft, the *Kon-Leekki*, in to land.

"Hello, Thør," said Minty Woodvine, joining them on the shore. She'd just reflanged the flange bolt and was taking a break before unspatching the spatch lock. "Ottoline and her assistant here are travelling to Norway. Can you give them a lift?" she asked.

131

"Certainly," said Thør, looking at Ottoline's Amateur Roving Collectors' travel pass. "All aboard!"

"My best friend, Mr. Munroe, has gone missing," Ottoline explained to Thør. "He's small and hairy and comes from a bog in Norway."

Thør Thørrensen stroked his yellow beard thoughtfully. "I think I might just be able to help," he said with a smile.

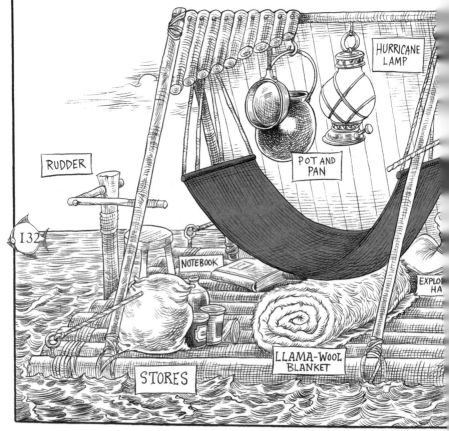

HURRICANE LAMP

POT AND PAN

RUDDER

132

NOTEBOOK

EXPLO
HA

LLAMA-WOOL BLANKET

STORES

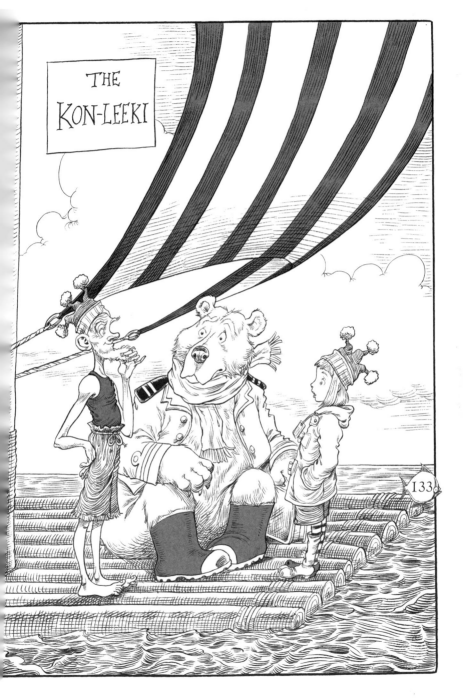

THE
KON-LEEKI

133

Chapter Nine

"I first perfected the Whistle of the Wild on my hot-air-balloon tour of the South Seas," said Thør Thørrensen as they sailed away, "when a passing albatross saved me from a volcano. Then, in South America, I met some very helpful llamas . . ."

"Yes!" said Ottoline. "You whistled and they carried you over the Andes. That's Mr. Munroe's favourite bit in your book." She sighed.

Thør put three fingers in his mouth and blew. Ottoline couldn't hear a thing, but the bear covered his ears.

"Ooo-wwwwww!" he yelped.

A few moments later two sea turtles surfaced next to the *Kon-Leekki*, followed by a large whale. Then a sea eagle appeared and dropped down on to the mast.

"Given a lift to anyone small and hairy recently?" asked Thør.

The turtles nodded, the eagle gave a screech and the whale blew water out of its blowhole.

"Can you show us where he went?" asked Ottoline.

The *Kon-Leekki* sliced through the waves until they came to the coast of Norway. Then they followed the creatures of the wild up a narrow fjord.

"My parents are looking for Quite Big Foot the Abominable Troll, and I think Mr. Munroe has gone to help them," said Ottoline. "He might be shy. But he's rather brave and quite helpful too. He—"

"Quite Big Foot!" exclaimed Thør, shaking his head, "Why he's . . ."

"I know," said Ottoline. "*Eight feet tall, snaggle-toothed and with a terrible temper and huge claws, sticking-up hair, eyes as big as headlamps . . .*"

"And quite big feet," added Thør. "At least, that's what they say."

137

At the end of the fjord Thør helped Ottoline
and the bear ashore and gave a whistle.

EXPLORER'S
HAT

MINTY WOODVINE'S
SCARF

CAPTAIN
PASTERNAK'S
JACKET

SUITCASE
CONTAINING
HIMALAYAN
RAINHOOD,
PATAGONIAN
PONCHO AND
HAIRBRUSH

BOGTROTTERS

The bear took a photograph of Ottoline
standing with Thør Thørrensen.

"May I have your autograph too, please?"
she said, blushing. "It's for Mr. Munroe.
When I find him."

Captain Pasternak

Minty Woodvine

OTTOLINE'S NOTEBOOK

Thor Thorrensen

139

Just then a mountain goat trotted up.

"Ninian, at your service," he said. "How can I help?"

"Would you be so kind as to give my friends here a lift over the mountain to the bog on the other side?" asked Thør Thørrensen politely.

Ninian looked the bear up and down. "I'll need some help . . . Bradley!" he bellowed.

A large, shaggy Norwegian mountain ox came clip-clopping down the mountainside.

"Meet Bradley," said Ninian.

Thør waved goodbye. "Happy roving!" he called, readying the *Kon-Leekki* to set sail.

141

Chapter Ten

Ottoline, the bear, Ninian and Bradley travelled all the way to the top of the mountain. And all the way down the other side. When they got to the edge of the bog Ninian and Bradley stopped.

"Are you sure you want to go on?" asked Ninian. "It's cold and wet. And I've heard this is where Quite Big Foot the Abominable Troll lives. Apparently he's—"

"We know!" said Ottoline breezily. She turned to the bear. "Ready?"

"Ready," the bear said. He was shaking a bit but it didn't show under his Himalayan rainhood.

"Rather you than me," muttered Bradley.

Ottoline and the bear trudged through the bog. It was cold . . .

. . . and wet. Then it began to rain.

They didn't see anyone anywhere.

Then Ottoline heard a muffled sneeze. And then another. Following the sound, she came to a hole. In the bottom of the hole were two small, hairy Norwegian bog people.

"Good day," said Ottoline politely. "You haven't, by any chance, seen any Professional Roving Collectors passing through lately?"

The bog people shook their heads.

"What about a small, hairy bog person called Mr. Munroe?" she asked.

One of the bog people pointed.

Ottoline looked down and saw a trail of footprints.

"Mr. Munroe!" she gasped.

It continued to rain . . .

... heavily.

The footprints led into a deep, dark cave.
"I don't like caves," muttered the bear.
"I much prefer basements and cupboards . . ."
"Follow me," whispered Ottoline.

150

155

Ottoline stared at Quite Big Foot. He was huge and he did have quite big feet, but he wasn't scary at all. In fact, he looked rather shy.

"Are you the reason Mr. Munroe came to Norway?" she asked.

Quite Big Foot nodded his shaggy head.

"But why didn't you tell me?" Ottoline said, turning to Mr. Munroe.

Mr. Munroe handed Ottoline the glasses he'd borrowed from Ottoline's parents' collection.

Ottoline put them on . . .

DR. J. T. ECKLEBERG'S "BOG GOGGLES" HELP THE WEARER TO SEE THINGS MORE CLEARLY

. . . and saw things more clearly.

159

"Oh, Mr. Munroe. I'm so sorry!"
Ottoline flung her arms around
Mr. Munroe and hugged him tight.
"I'll never ignore you again!"

"This cave reminds me of my cave in Canada,"
said the bear, looking around. "Cold and
damp and miles away from anywhere — no
wonder Quite Big Foot looks miserable.

"You should do what I did," he told Quite
Big Foot, "and take a holiday."

"But don't you see? He *can't* go on holiday," said Ottoline. "That's the trouble. He's Quite Big Foot the Abominable Troll of Trondheim — troll spotters are out looking for him, telling stories about how big and fierce and scary he is . . ."

Quite Big Foot nodded his shaggy head sadly.

"They'll track him down," said Ottoline.

Quite Big Foot nodded.

"And point and stare and take photographs . . ." Ottoline went on.

A big tear ran down Quite Big Foot's hairy cheek.

"Unless . . ." Ottoline smiled.

"You look fabulous," said the bear.

"Unrecognizable," said Ottoline.

Mr. Munroe nodded and Quite Big Foot smiled.

"I don't know how you do it, Ottoline," said the bear.

"Simple – with a little help from my friends," said Ottoline, "and a clever plan."

"MR. ABERCROMBIE"

THØR THØRRENSSEN'S EXPLORER'S HAT

MINTY WOODVINE'S SCARF

THE BEAR'S HIMALAYAN RAINHOOD AND PATAGONIAN PONCHO

CAPTAIN PASTERNAK'S SECOND-BEST JACKET

OTTOLINE'S ROVE O'MATIC CAMERA

CANADIAN SOCKS

THE POLAR BEAR SHOE Cº'S BOG TROTTERS

165

Back in Big City, Ottoline sat down on the Beidermeyer sofa with Mr. Munroe and kicked off her odd shoes. "You might come from a cold, wet bog in Norway," she said, "but I hope you know your home will always be here with me."

Mr. Munroe didn't say anything. He just shuffled a little bit closer to Ottoline and handed her the postcard that he'd found on the welcome mat.

167

168

Dearest O,
What a pity we missed each other in Norway! You're quite a roving collector now. Pa and I are very proud and think it's time you and Mr. Munroe joined us on a collecting trip. We are on our way home,
lots of love,
Ma.

P.S. We never did find Quite Big Foot!

P.P.S. Don't forget to put the bog goggles back.

TRONDHEIM
13·04·10
NORWAY

2kr

Miss O. Brown,

Apartment 243,

The Pepperpot Bld.,

3rd Street,

BIG CITY,

3001

169

First published 2010 by Macmillan Children's Books
a division of Macmillan Publishers Limited
20 New Wharf Road, London N1 9RR
Basingstoke and Oxford
Associated companies throughout the world
www.panmacmillan.com

ISBN 978-1-4050-5059-3

Printed and bound in China
1 3 5 7 9 8 6 4 2